Garuda

The Eagle Who Soared with Ahimsa

Ally Ford

Illustrated by *Eduardo Micardi*

For my angels, Ian and Ila. -A.F.

Garuda the Eagle lived high in the sky
in the tall mountains where only he could fly.

But he longed for some friends – he was lonely up there
with no one to talk to and no one to share.

He tried to make friends but when he flew near the others would run or hide out of fear.

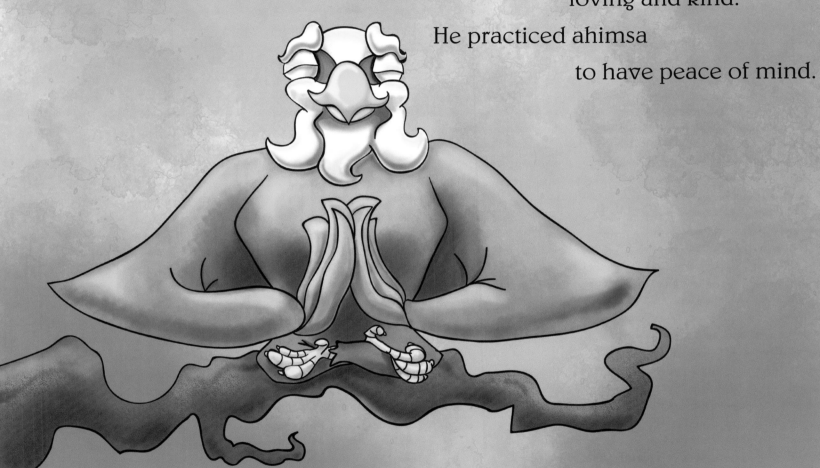

But Garuda was gentle,
        loving and kind.
He practiced ahimsa
        to have peace of mind.

No harm to others is ahimsa, you see
and this was how Garuda aimed to be.

So he promised to try and no longer postpone
making new friends so he wasn't alone.

From the highest tree branch

he peered through the skies

and took flight like a plane with his eyes on the prize.

He spied a fair cat on a stroll through the woods
and landed beside her as softly as he could.

Cat arched her back,

all her hairs stood on end.

Garuda said softly, "Can I be your friend?"

"I look fierce, but don't judge this book by its cover.
I live with ahimsa and vow not to harm others."

To welcome her friend Cat showed him how to roll and meow when up walked a cow!

Cow was surprised to see such a sight.

A bird and a cat? It just didn't seem right.

With joy, Garuda said, "There's nothing wrong.
Please join our group and we'll all get along!"

"Cat and I are doing no harm.

Ahimsa's our vow...no cause for alarm."

So Cow joined in and taught them his ways,
like milking and mooing and of course how to graze!

Tired from playing they napped by a log.

And soon were awakened by a curious dog.

Now, Dog loved new friends and he wasn't afraid
to join in the group so everyone played!

The gang started running and jumping around.

Dog taught them to stretch face up and face down.

Thirsty, the friends went to drink from the lake.

As they bowed their heads, up popped a snake!

Snake hissed a warning out of pure fright,
"Please keep your distance. I fear I will bite!

Rather than love me and treat me sweetly,
I have been taught that an eagle would eat me!"

Then Cat told Snake of Garuda's vow
and invited him along so he could learn how
to practice non-harming and treat others with love,
a vow that made Eagle as sweet as a dove.

So Snake taught his friends to slither and hiss
and play hide and seek, a game not to miss.

When soon the sun started going down
Garuda said, "Friends, please gather around."

"Thank you for playing. It is time I must go.
There's something important I want you to know.
Our friendships are off to a promising start.
Your smiles and laughter have healed my heart."

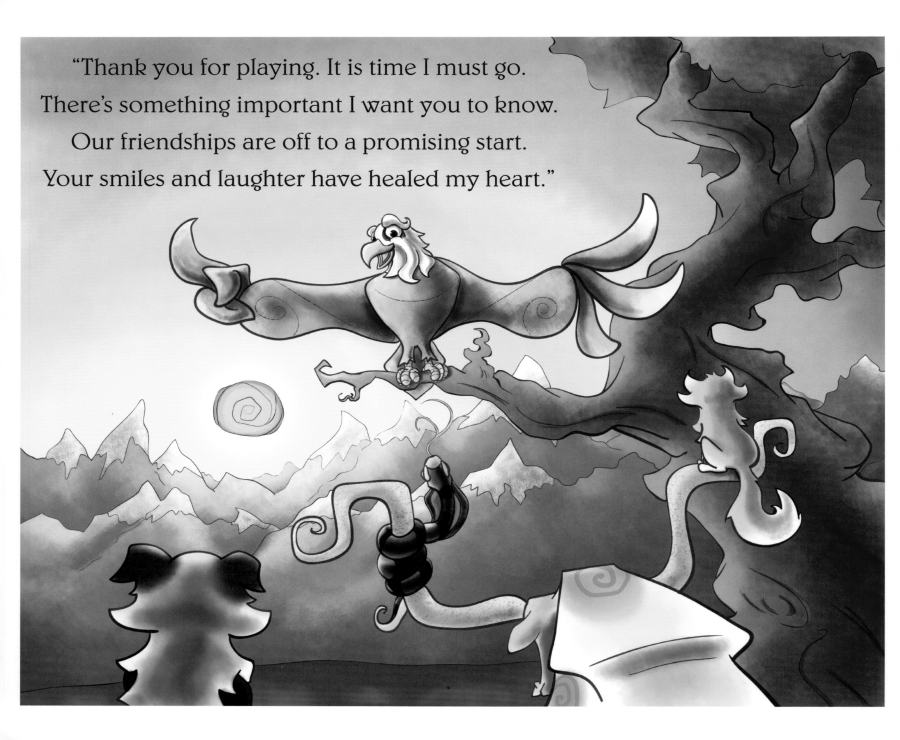

"I'm no longer lonely high up in my tree,
because I know you will be thinking of me.
Run and jump and explore this grand world
and share all the treasures your hearts will unfurl."

"Be grateful for all of the things that you have.

If you think of them daily, it will make you feel glad.

I will fly by often and promise you this,

there's no need to fear so live life in bliss!"

"Treat each other with kindness and you'll always be
full of joy, happy and...

f r e e."

Author's Note

When I began teaching yoga to kindergarten and first grade students at my children's school, it just made sense to incorporate some of the deeper lessons given to us by the Yoga Sutras of Patanjali, especially ahimsa. Ahimsa, or nonviolence, is one of the five yamas—ethical principles for how we treat others and our environment. We made up songs about being gentle, loving, and kind and discussed what it would mean to treat our friends this way. The children were very receptive to this message. Out of our playful classes came this story—a story of how an animal that might normally eat other animals decided to practice non-harming and treat others with love.

As an animal lover, I asked Eduardo Micardi to base the animal designs on those I have known and loved throughout life. Garuda the Eagle is modeled after my favorite bird, the majestic Bald Eagle. Cat was inspired by my neighbor's snuggly, adorable cat, "Calico" who meows sweetly when she sees me in my yard, comes when called and with whom I feel I can literally hold a conversation. Cow is a Longhorn, of course, the mascot of my alma matter, The University of Texas at Austin and a tribute to my home state of Texas. Snake, a cobra, represents my fondness of India where I studied yoga. And last but not least, Dog is a semblance of my beloved Border Collie, Sam (aka Wonder Dog), the smartest, sweetest dog that ever lived, with whom I shared some of my happiest memories over 12 incredible years, and who will forever live on in my heart.

I hope the message of Ahimsa inspires playful and meaningful conversation between parents and caregivers and their children.

Text copyright © 2013 by Ally Ford
Illustrations copyright © 2013 by Eduardo Micardi. Photos by Miranda Sears.
All rights reserved. No part of this book may be reproduced or transmitted in any form without written permission from the author.
Text for this book is set in Belwe.
Illustrations for this book were created with digital wizardy.
Library of Congress-in-Publication Data
Ford, Ally , 1971-
TXu001881731 2013
Garuda, The Eagle Who Soared With Ahimsa. / by Ally Ford;
illustrated by Eduardo Micardi.
ISBN 978-0-578-14637-9

Yoga Poses

Ahimsa

Tree Pose

Eagle Pose

Mountain Pose

Yoga Poses

Upward Facing Dog Pose

Downward Facing Dog Pose

Snake (Cobra) Pose

Cat Pose

Cow Pose